GRAPHIC MYTHICAL CREATURES

VAMPIRES

BY GARY JEFFREY

ILLUSTRATED BY DHEERAJ VERMA

Gareth Stevens
Publishing

Please visit our website, www.garethstevens.com.
For a free color catalog of all our high-quality books,
call toll free 1-800-542-2595 or fax 1-877-542-2596.

Library of Congress Cataloging-in-Publication Data

Jeffrey, Gary.
Vampires / Gary Jeffrey.
p. cm. — (Graphic mythical creatures)
Includes index.
ISBN 978-1-4339-6773-3 (pbk.)
ISBN 978-1-4339-6774-0 (6-pack)
ISBN 978-1-4339-6771-9 (library binding)
1. Vampires. I. Title.
GR830.V3J42 2012
398.21—dc23

2011022746

First Edition

Published in 2012 by
Gareth Stevens Publishing
111 East 14th Street, Suite 349
New York, NY 10003

Designed by David West Books

Photo credits:
P4r, Antonio De Lorenzo; p5b, Ltshears

Printed in China

CPSIA compliance information: Batch #DW12GS: For further information contact Gareth Stevens, New York, New York at 1-800-542-2595.

CONTENTS

BLOOD SUCKERS

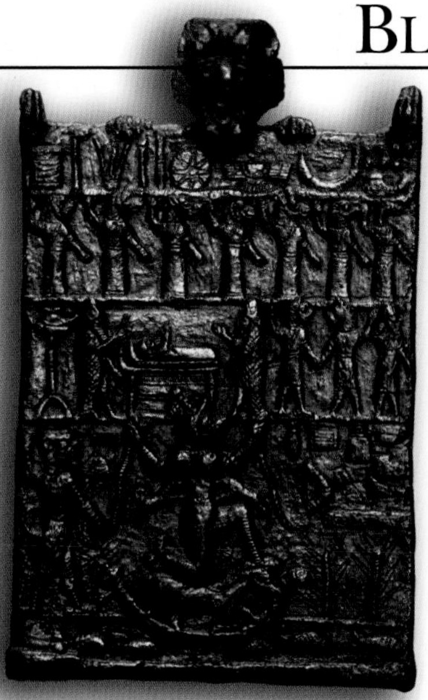

The shape-shifting, blood-sucking vampire has featured in worldwide folklore for centuries. Ancient vampires were terrifying half-human, half-animal demons who fed on the blood of babies and children.

This Iron Age tablet was made to ward off Lamashtu, an Assyrian vampire goddess.

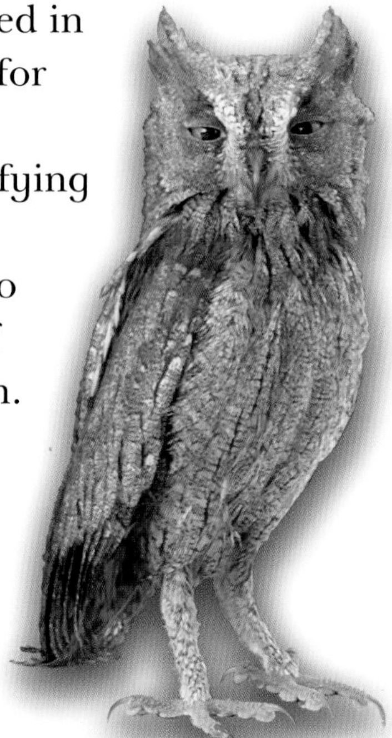

The Romans believed that the strix was a blood-drinking owl that was once a human.

TRANSYLVANIAN TERROR

The modern vampire was born in the Slavic countries of eastern Europe. The Slavs believed that if a person died suddenly and was unable to live the rest of their life, they would become one of the undead. When livestock or people died of mysterious causes, vampires were suspected of taking blood. The Slavs used crosses, holy water, and garlic to ward off vampires. Killing vampires by putting a stake through their heart also came from Slavic folklore.

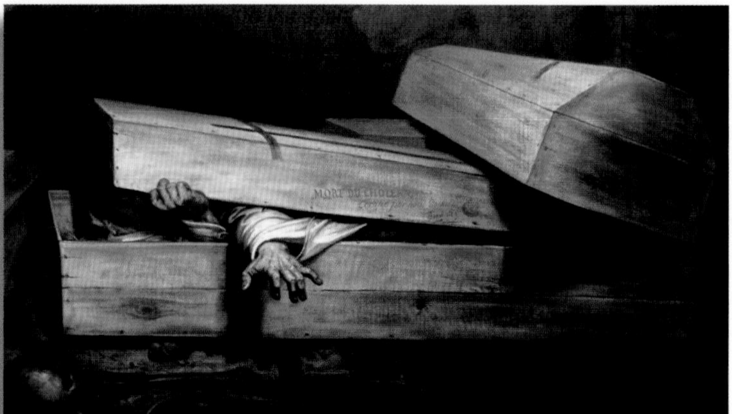

Bizarre cases of premature burial may also help to explain some vampire beliefs.

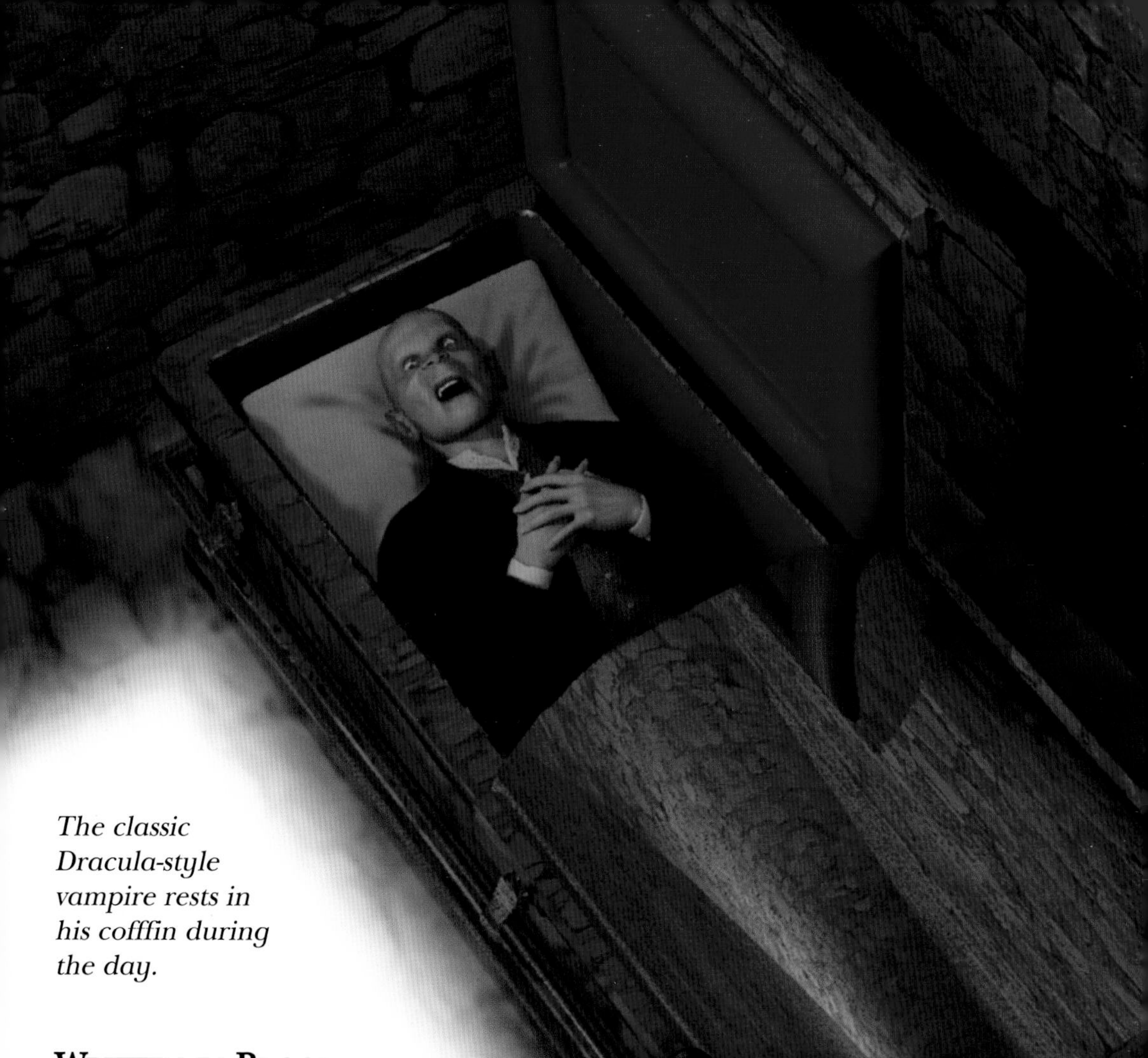

The classic Dracula-style vampire rests in his cofffin during the day.

WRITTEN IN BLOOD

There were many kinds of Slavic vampires, but an 1897 horror novel by Bram Stoker (which drew on Slavic myths and others) created a figure which put them all in the shade. A well-dressed man in evening clothes, fangs at the ready, *Dracula* has come to represent the danger and excitement of the fictional vampire.

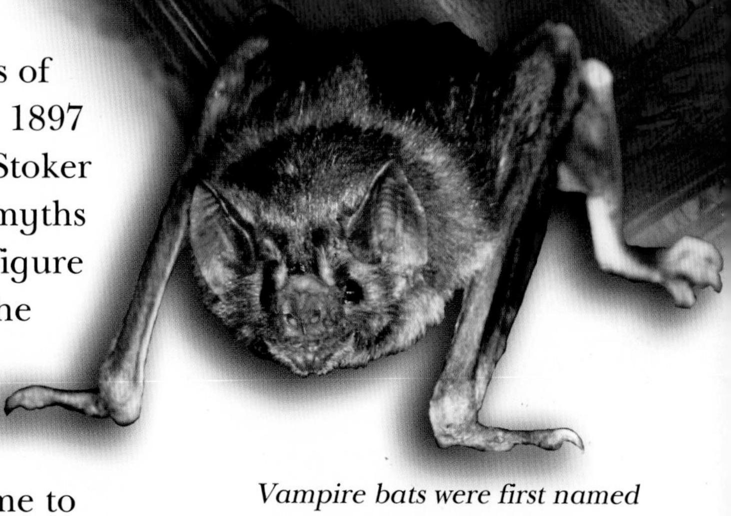

Vampire bats were first named by 16th-century Spanish explorers. Soon they, too, would become part of the legends.

ABHARTACH'S SEPULCHER

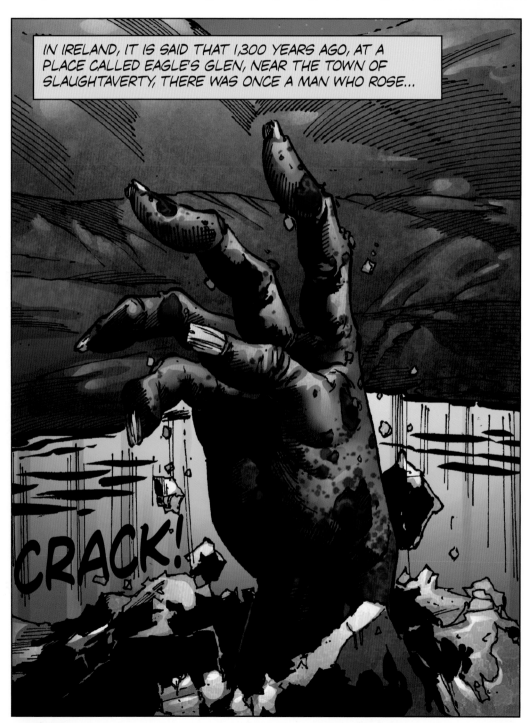

IN IRELAND, IT IS SAID THAT 1,300 YEARS AGO, AT A PLACE CALLED EAGLE'S GLEN, NEAR THE TOWN OF SLAUGHTAVERTY, THERE WAS ONCE A MAN WHO ROSE...

CRACK!

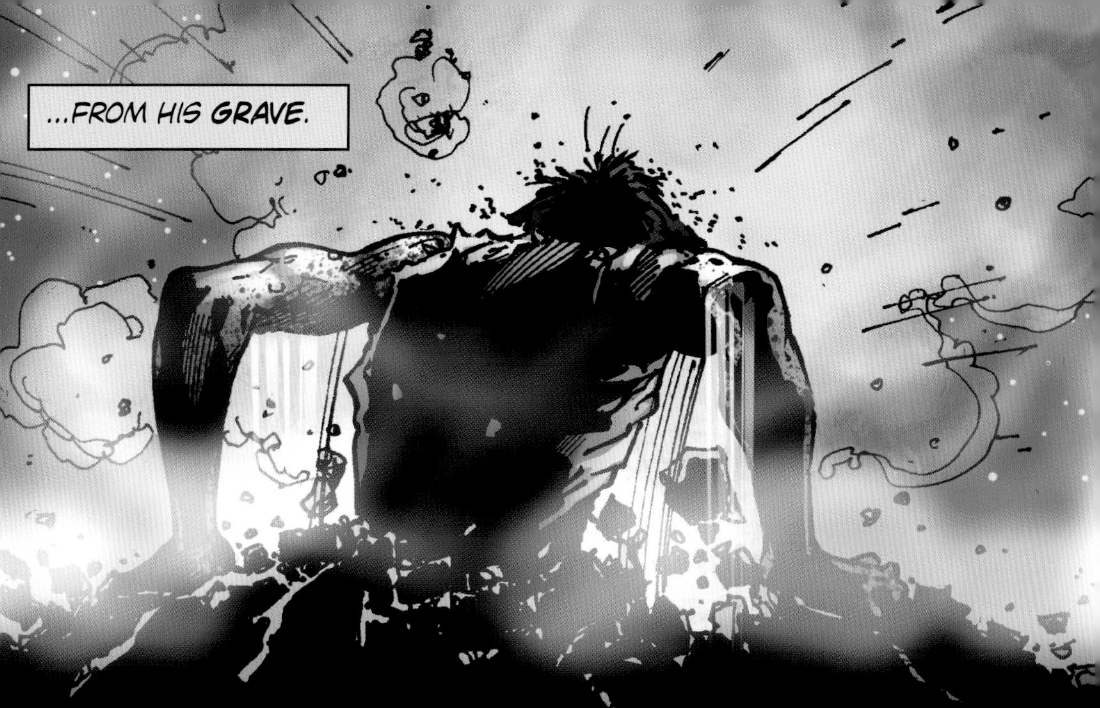
...FROM HIS GRAVE.

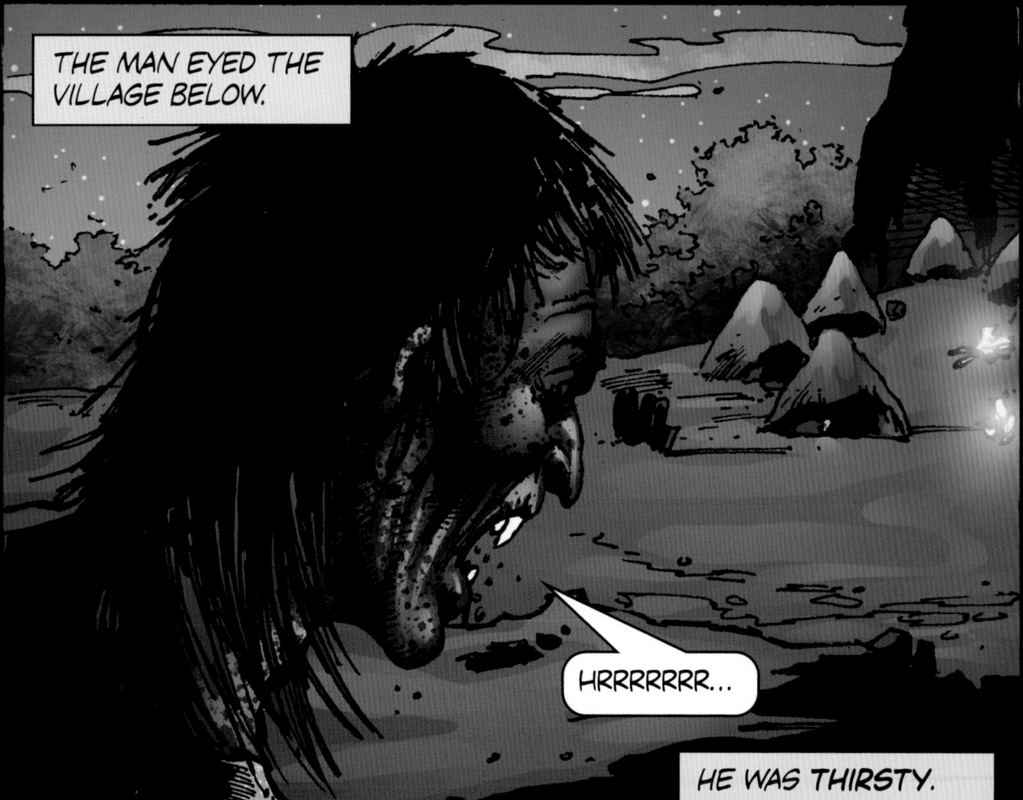
THE MAN EYED THE VILLAGE BELOW.
HRRRRRRR...
HE WAS THIRSTY.

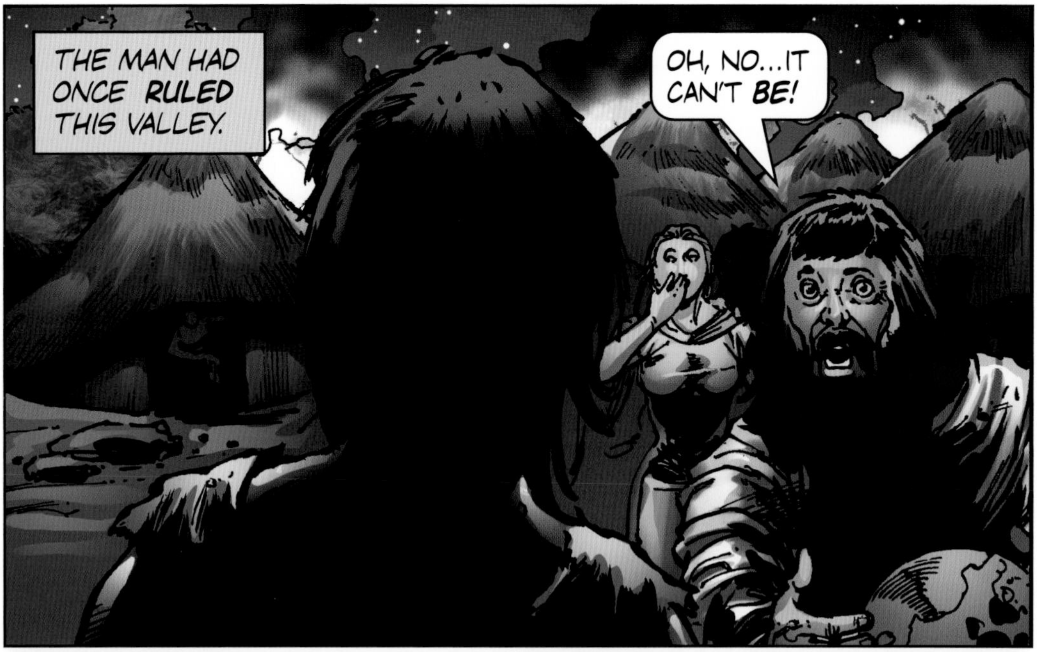
THE MAN HAD ONCE RULED THIS VALLEY.
OH, NO...IT CAN'T BE!

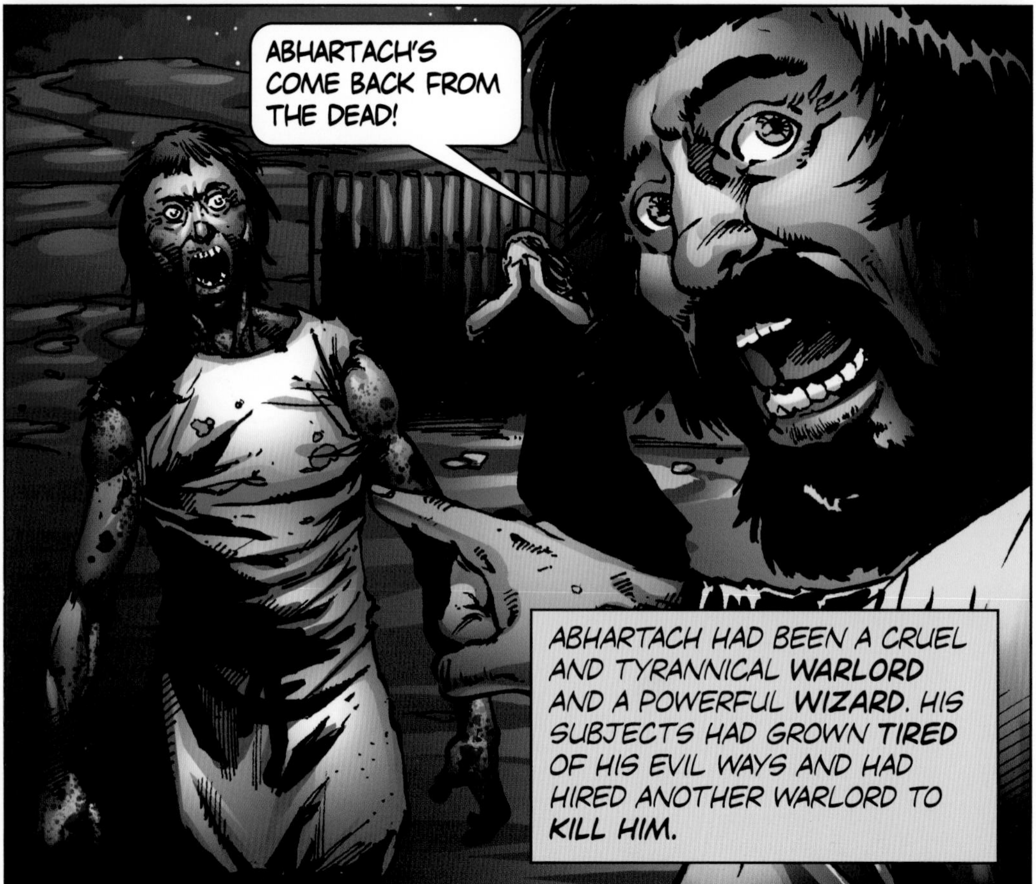
ABHARTACH'S COME BACK FROM THE DEAD!
ABHARTACH HAD BEEN A CRUEL AND TYRANNICAL WARLORD AND A POWERFUL WIZARD. HIS SUBJECTS HAD GROWN TIRED OF HIS EVIL WAYS AND HAD HIRED ANOTHER WARLORD TO KILL HIM.

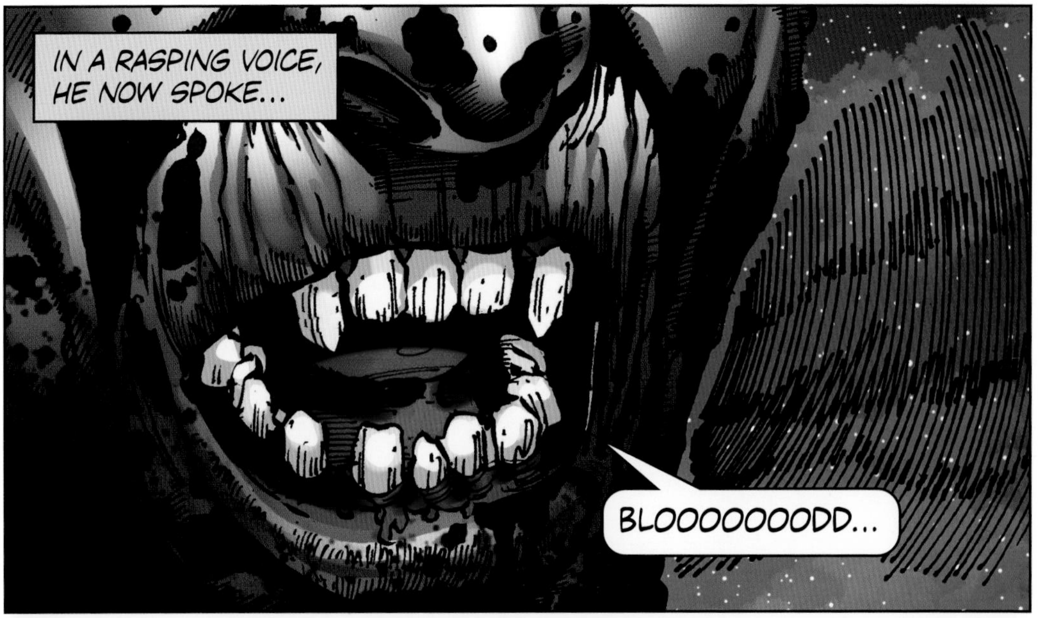
IN A RASPING VOICE, HE NOW SPOKE...
BLOOOOOOODD...

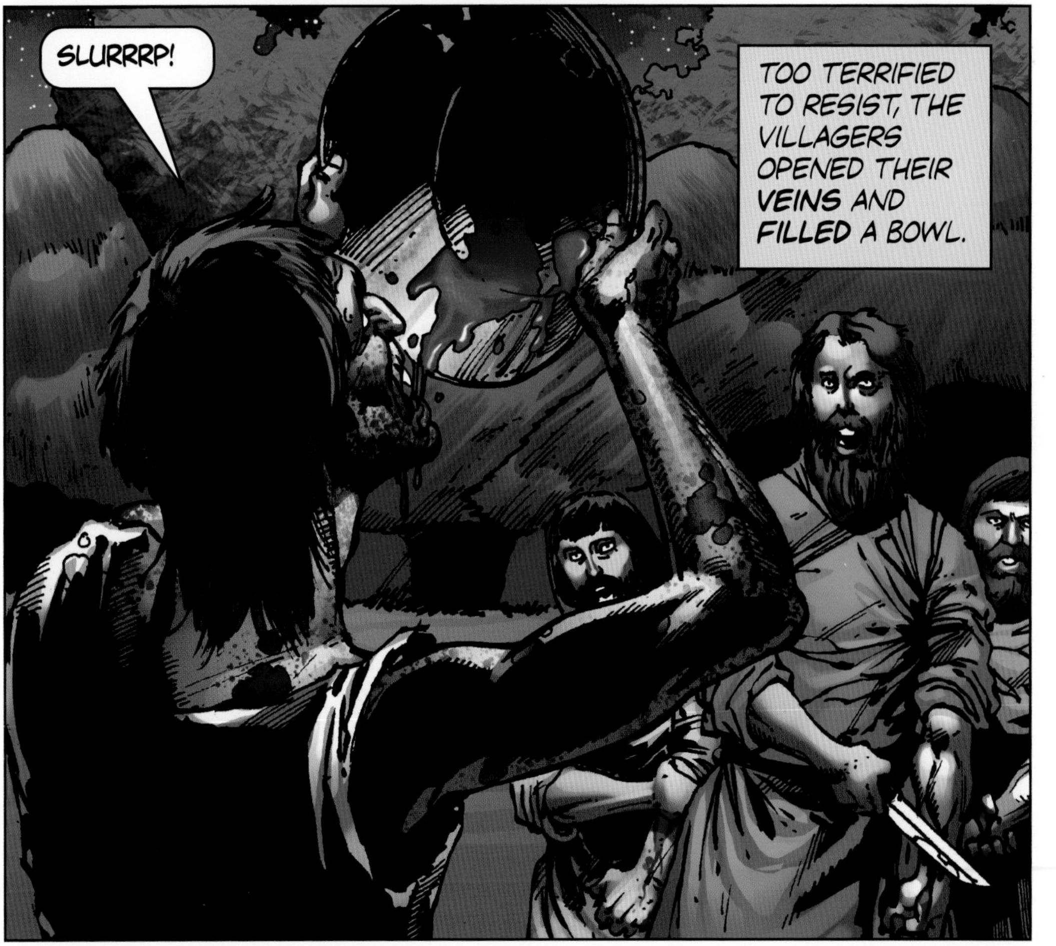
SLURRRP!
TOO TERRIFIED TO RESIST, THE VILLAGERS OPENED THEIR VEINS AND FILLED A BOWL.

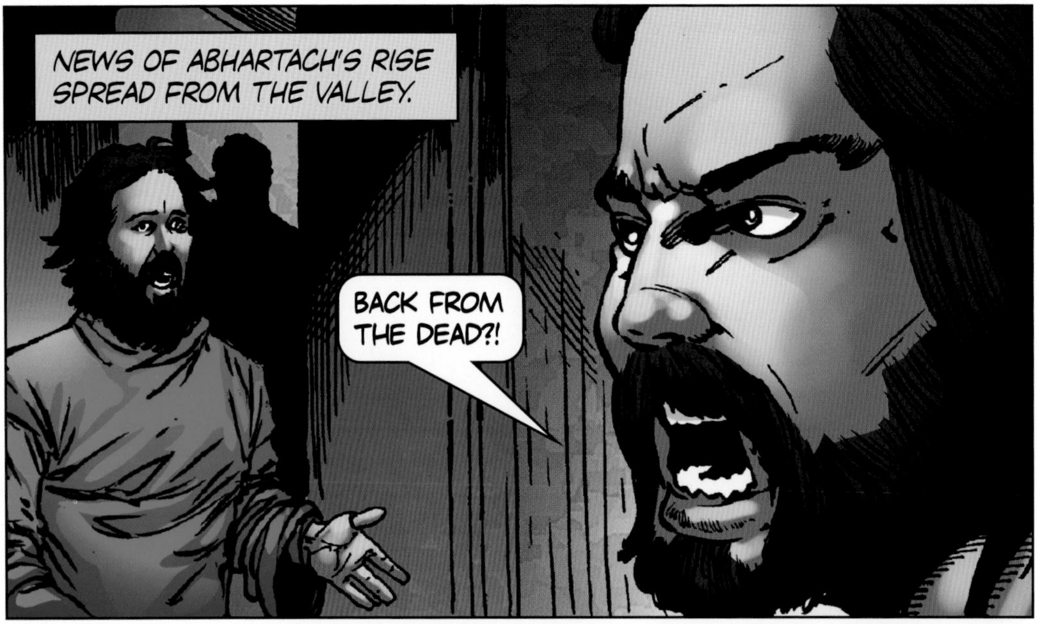
NEWS OF ABHARTACH'S RISE SPREAD FROM THE VALLEY.
BACK FROM THE DEAD?!

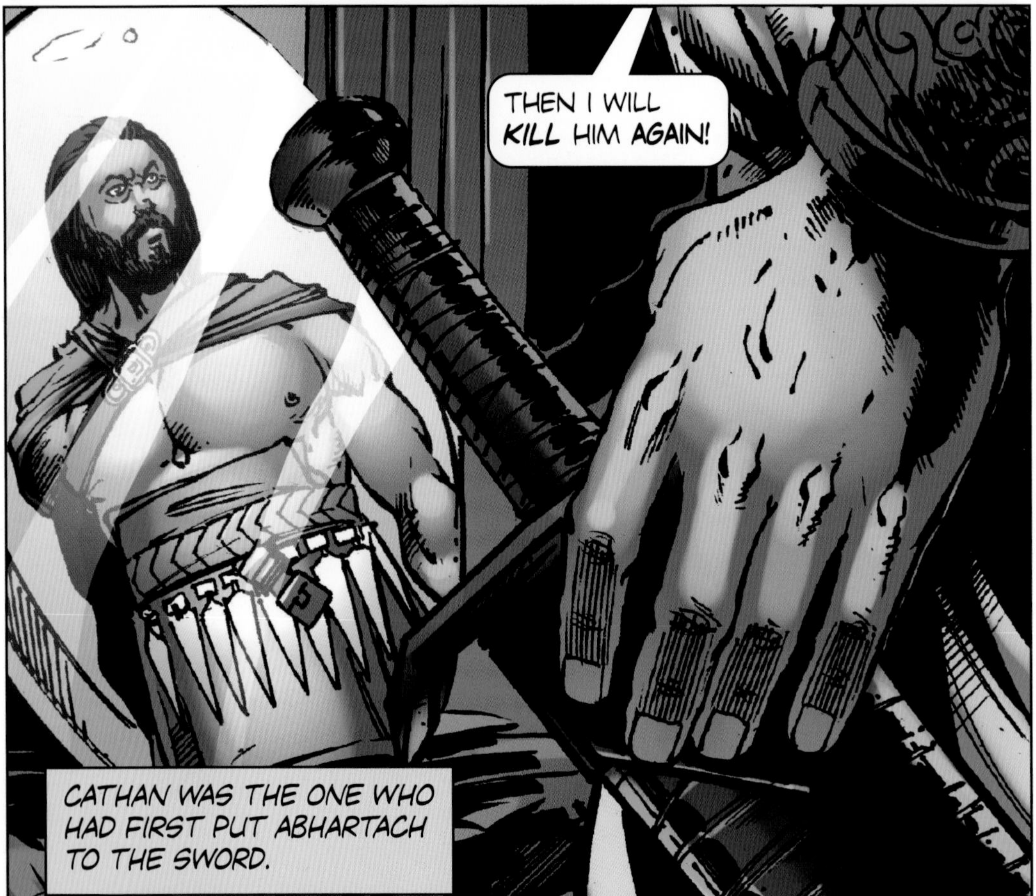
THEN I WILL KILL HIM AGAIN!
CATHAN WAS THE ONE WHO HAD FIRST PUT ABHARTACH TO THE SWORD.

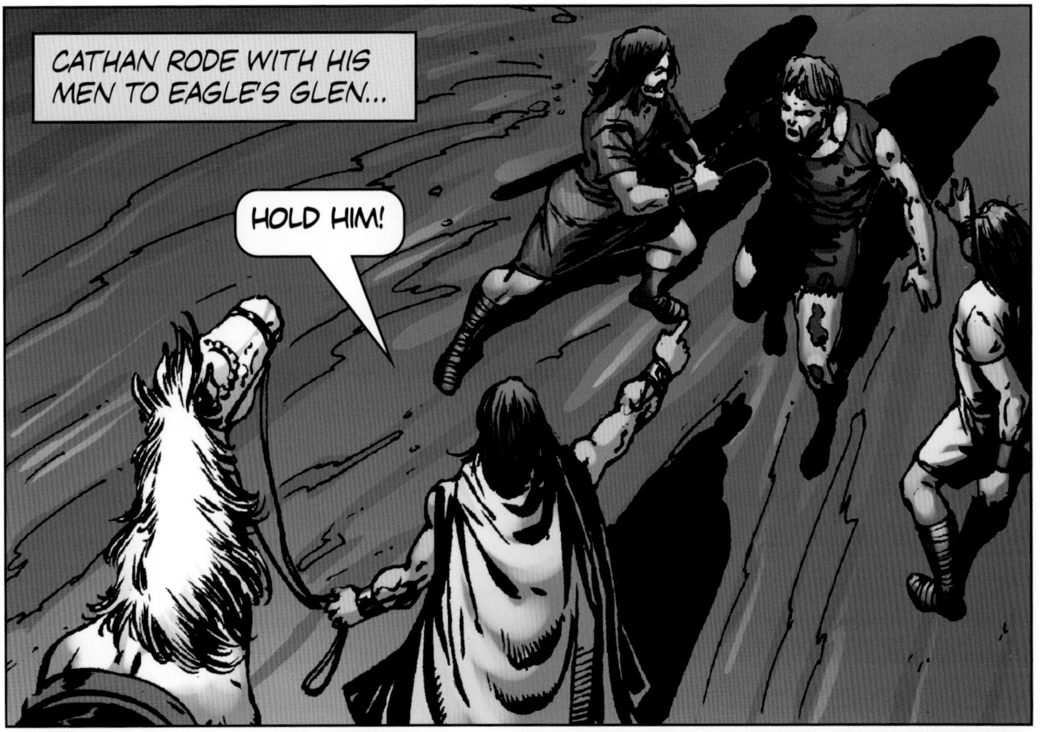
CATHAN RODE WITH HIS MEN TO EAGLE'S GLEN...
HOLD HIM!

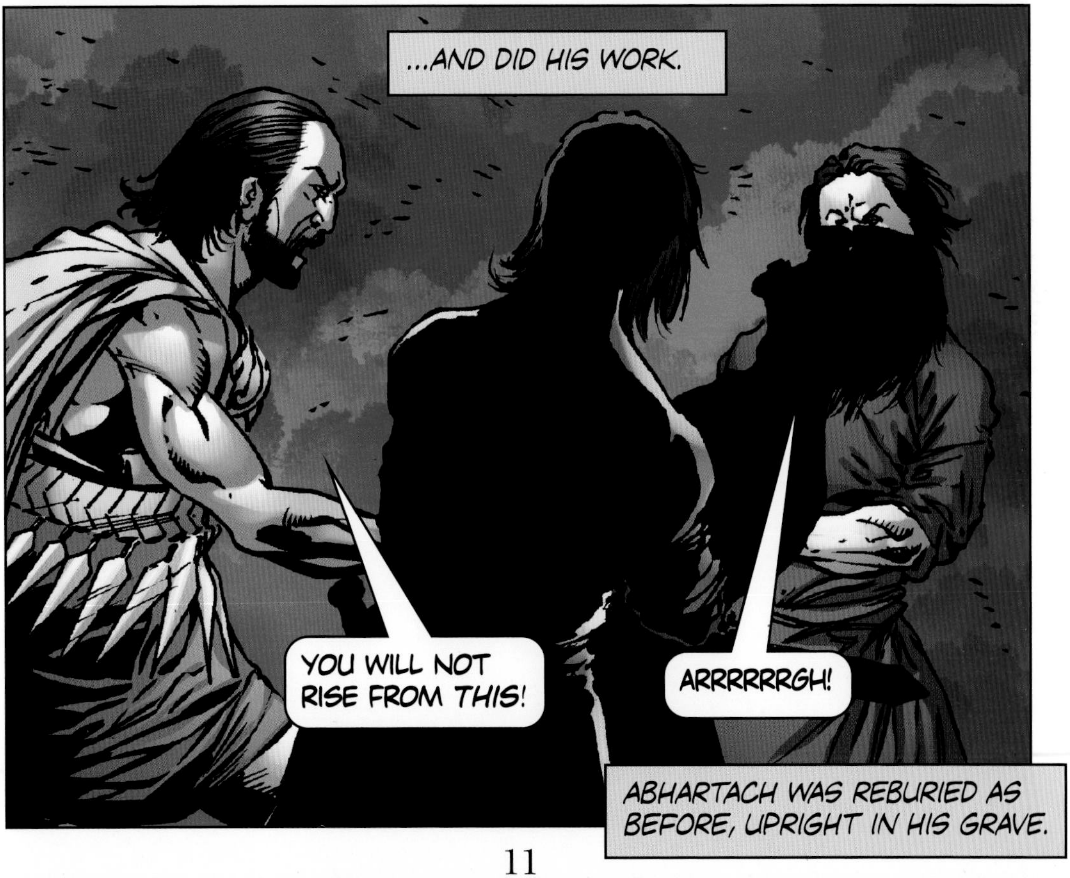
...AND DID HIS WORK.
YOU WILL NOT RISE FROM THIS!
ARRRRRRGH!
ABHARTACH WAS REBURIED AS BEFORE, UPRIGHT IN HIS GRAVE.

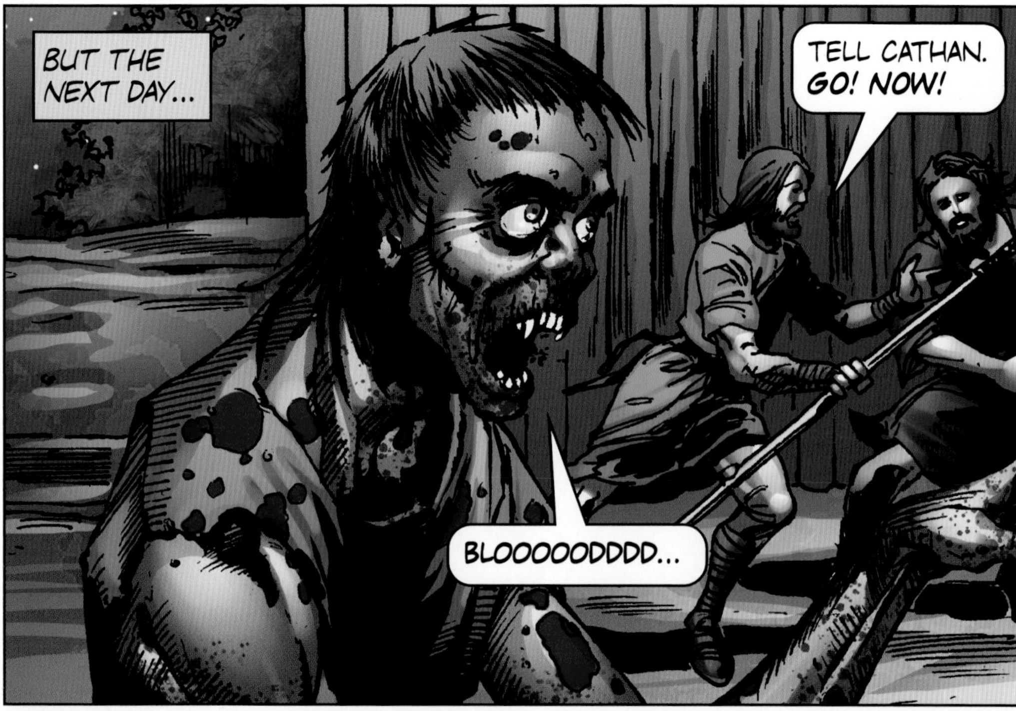
BUT THE NEXT DAY...
TELL CATHAN. GO! NOW!
BLOOOOODDDD...

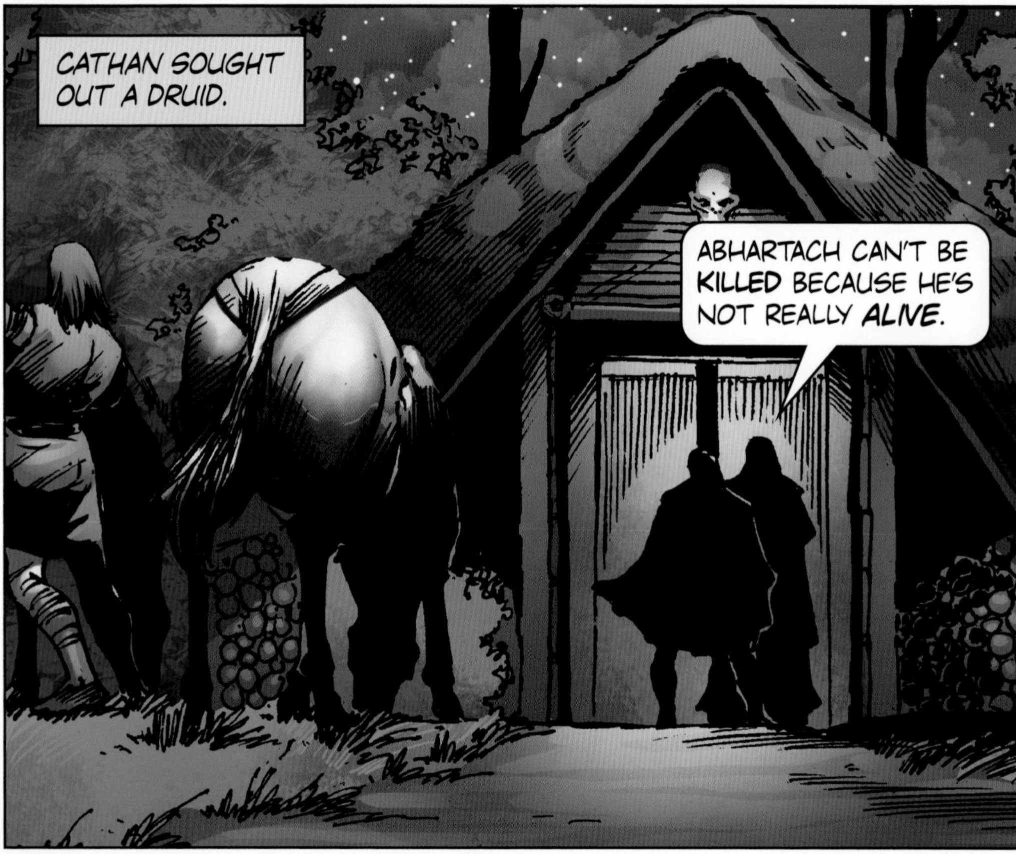
CATHAN SOUGHT OUT A DRUID.
ABHARTACH CAN'T BE KILLED BECAUSE HE'S NOT REALLY ALIVE.

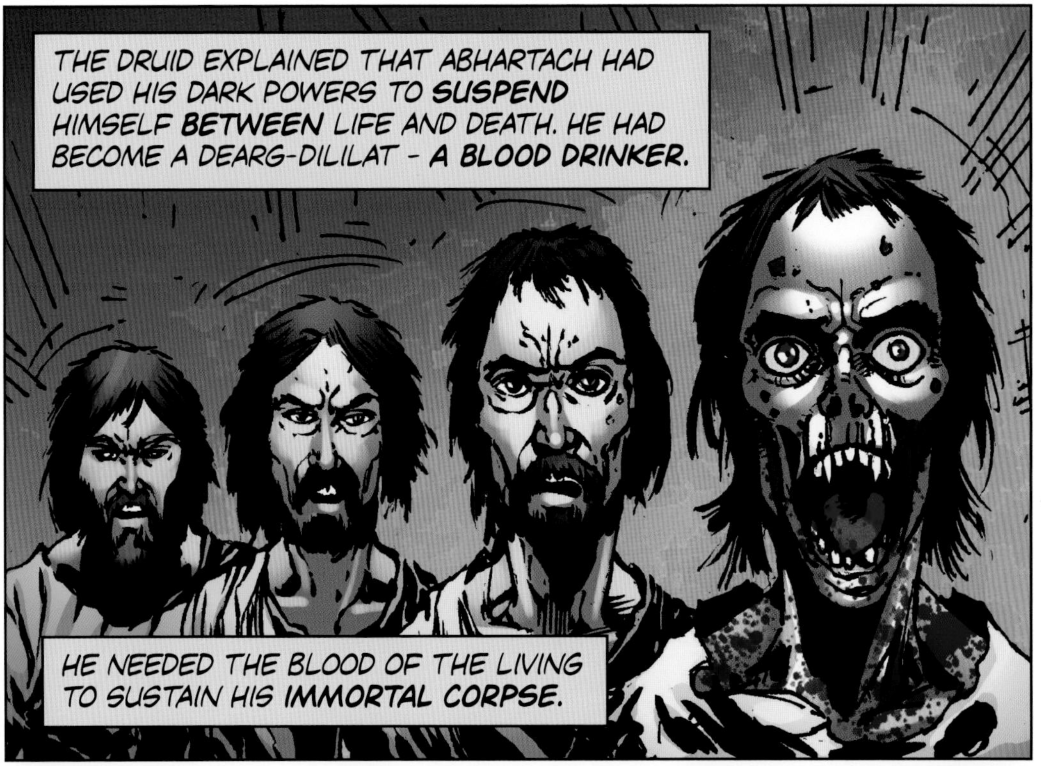
THE DRUID EXPLAINED THAT ABHARTACH HAD USED HIS DARK POWERS TO SUSPEND HIMSELF BETWEEN LIFE AND DEATH. HE HAD BECOME A DEARG-DILILAT - A BLOOD DRINKER.
HE NEEDED THE BLOOD OF THE LIVING TO SUSTAIN HIS IMMORTAL CORPSE.

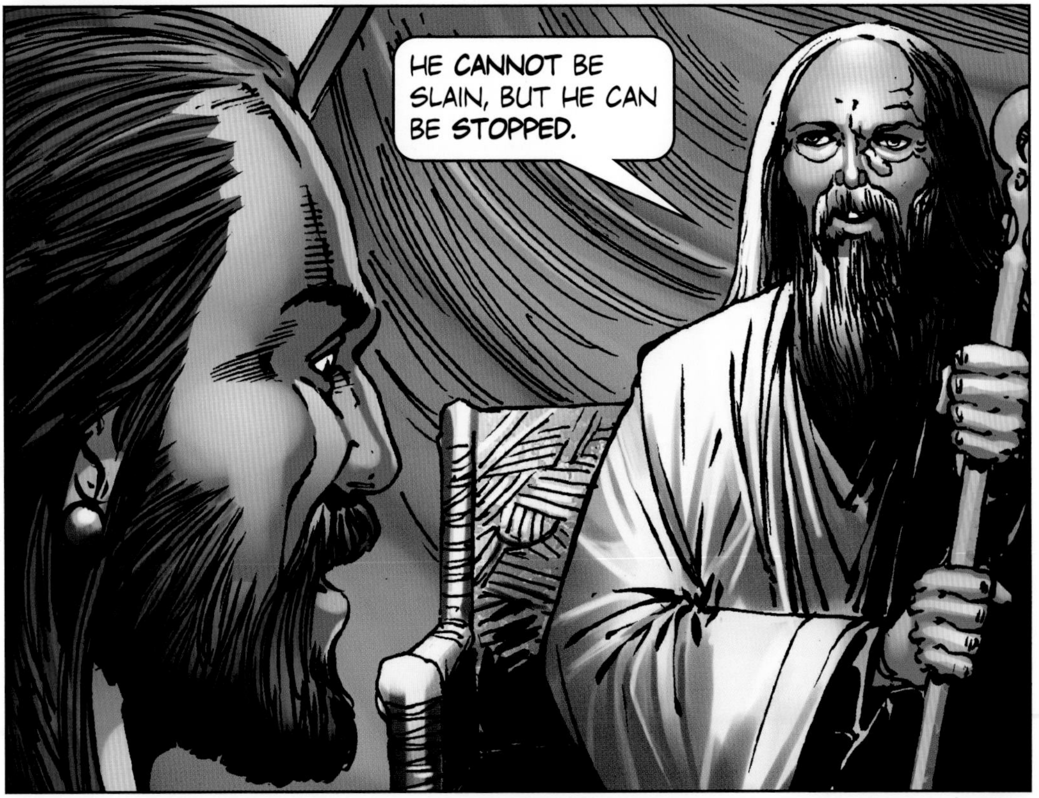
HE CANNOT BE SLAIN, BUT HE CAN BE STOPPED.

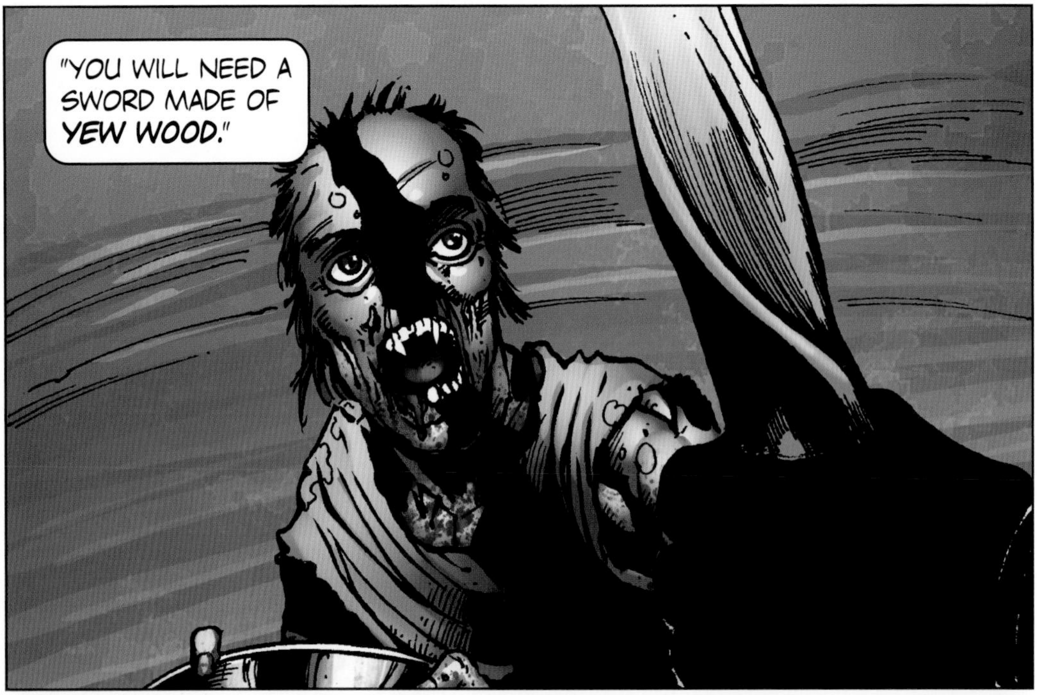
"YOU WILL NEED A SWORD MADE OF YEW WOOD."

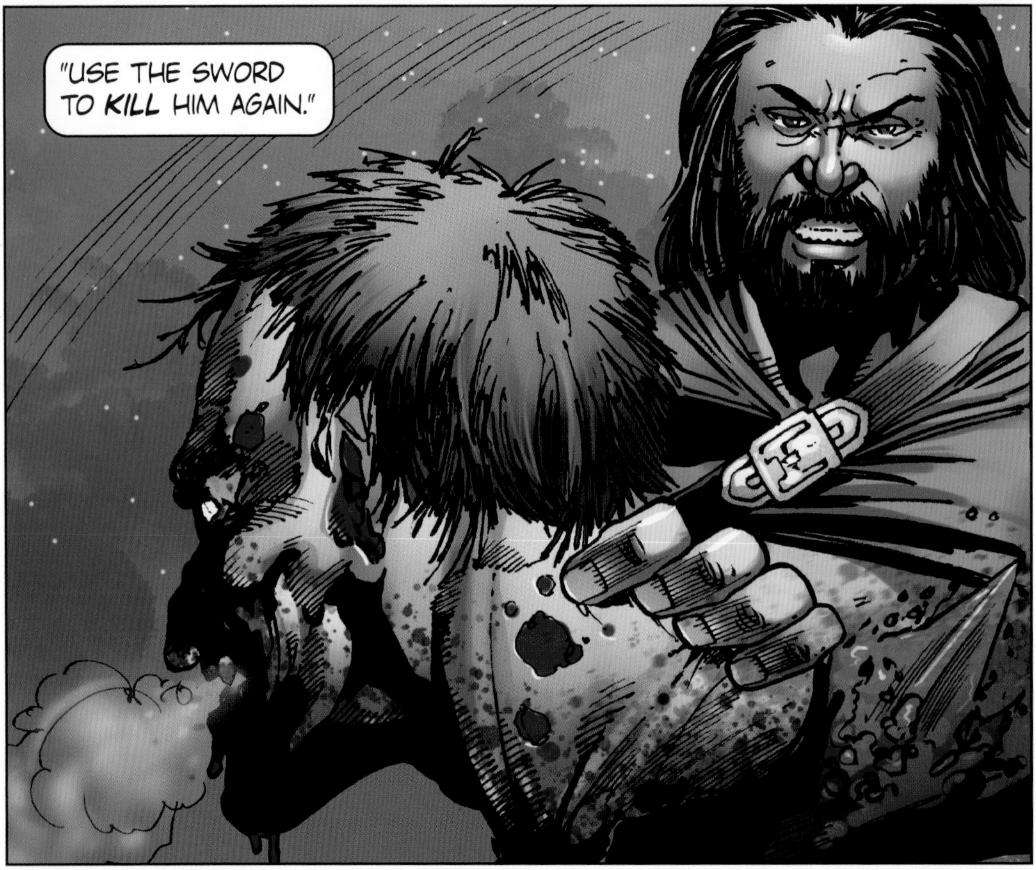
"USE THE SWORD TO KILL HIM AGAIN."

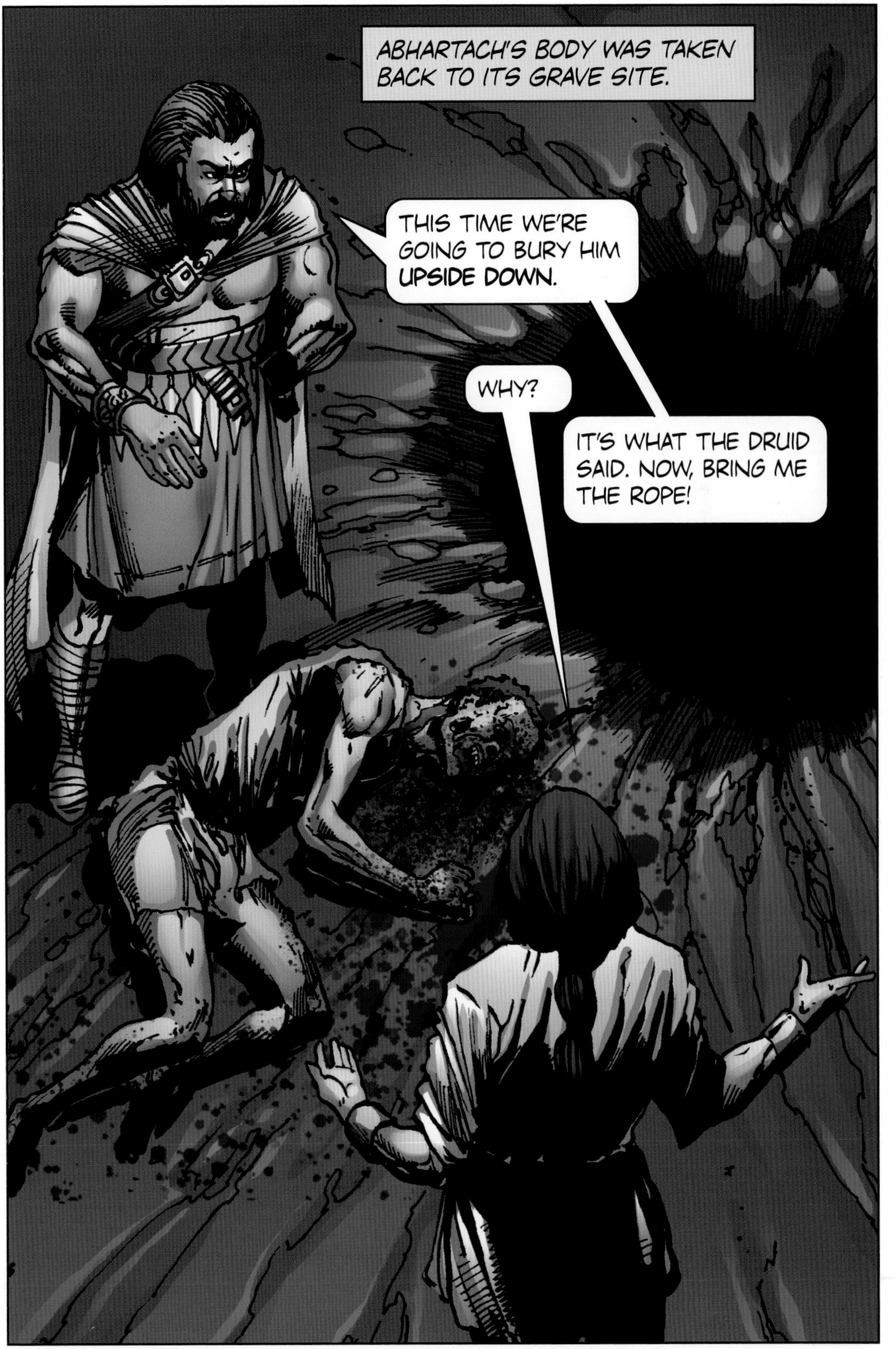
ABHARTACH'S BODY WAS TAKEN BACK TO ITS GRAVE SITE.
THIS TIME WE'RE GOING TO BURY HIM **UPSIDE DOWN.**
WHY?
IT'S WHAT THE DRUID SAID. NOW, BRING ME THE ROPE!

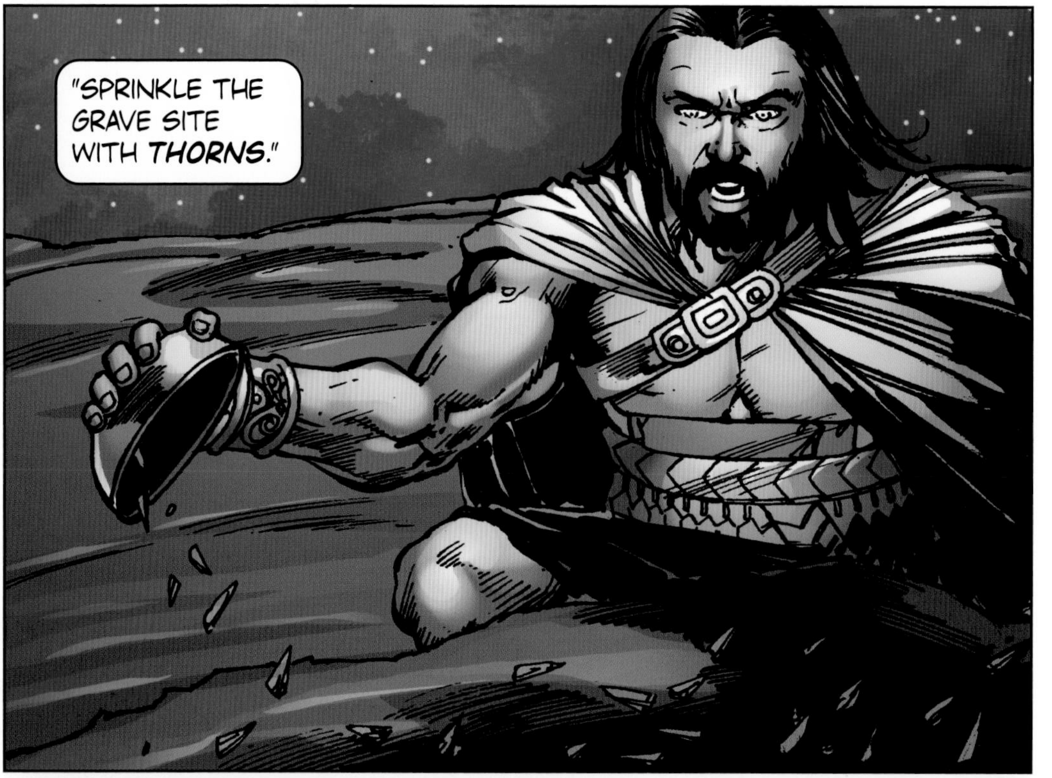
"SPRINKLE THE GRAVE SITE WITH **THORNS**."

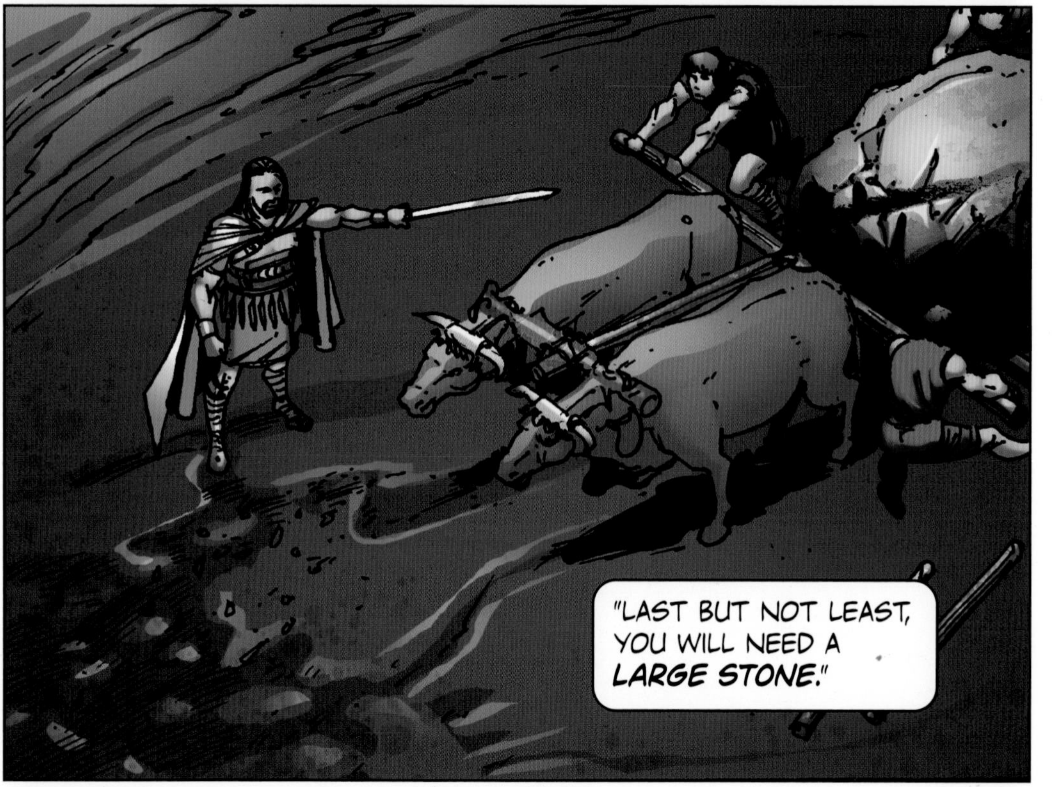
"LAST BUT NOT LEAST, YOU WILL NEED A **LARGE STONE**."

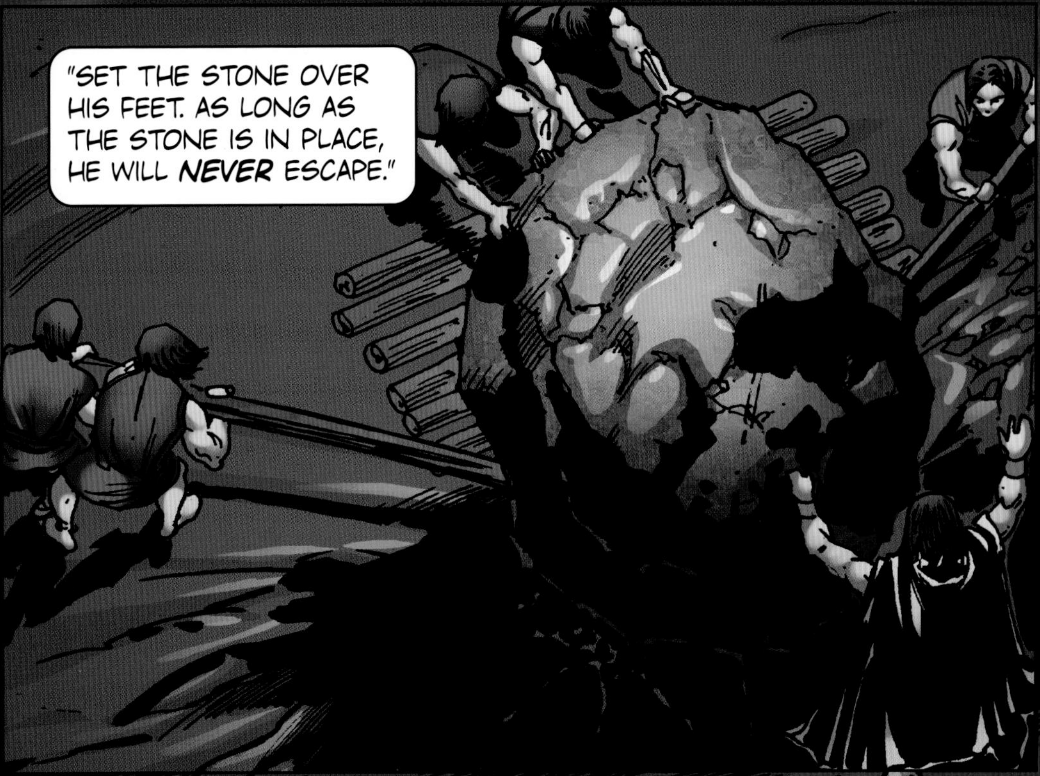
"SET THE STONE OVER HIS FEET. AS LONG AS THE STONE IS IN PLACE, HE WILL **NEVER** ESCAPE."

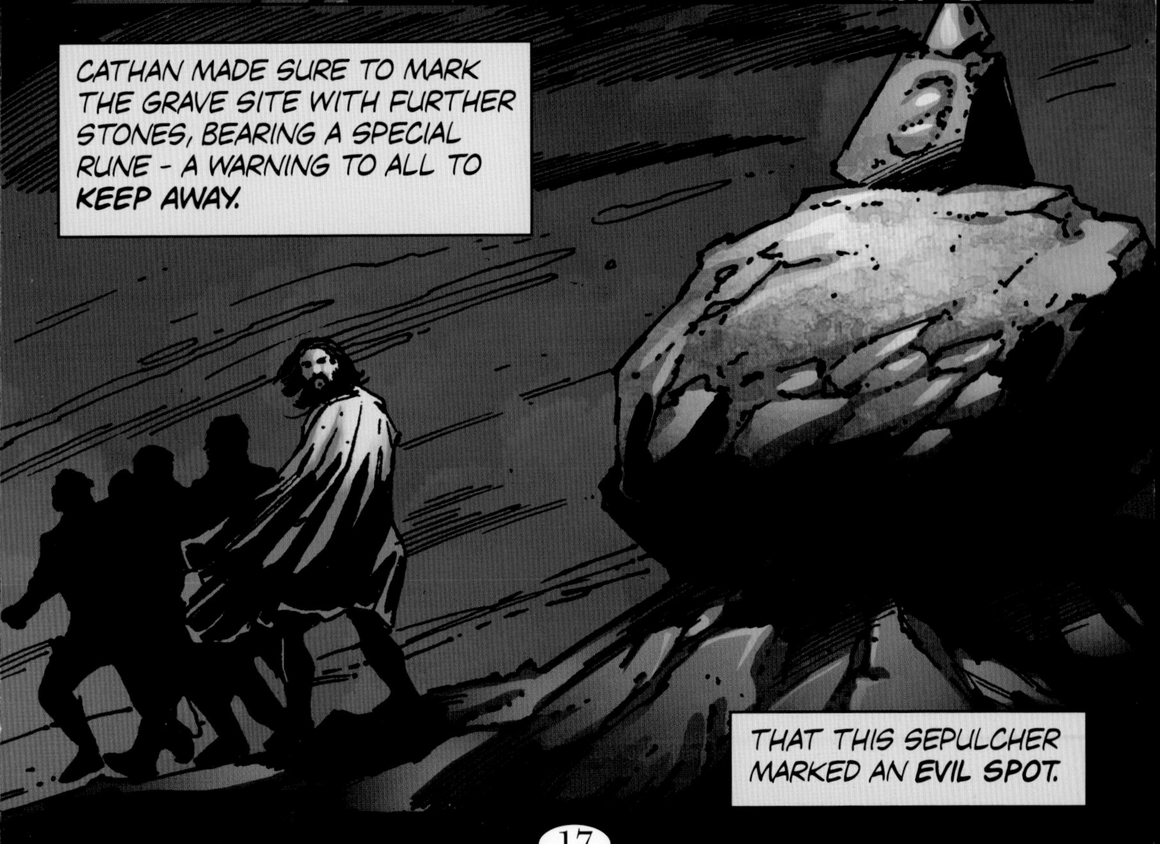
CATHAN MADE SURE TO MARK THE GRAVE SITE WITH FURTHER STONES, BEARING A SPECIAL RUNE - A WARNING TO ALL TO **KEEP AWAY.**
THAT THIS SEPULCHER MARKED AN **EVIL SPOT.**

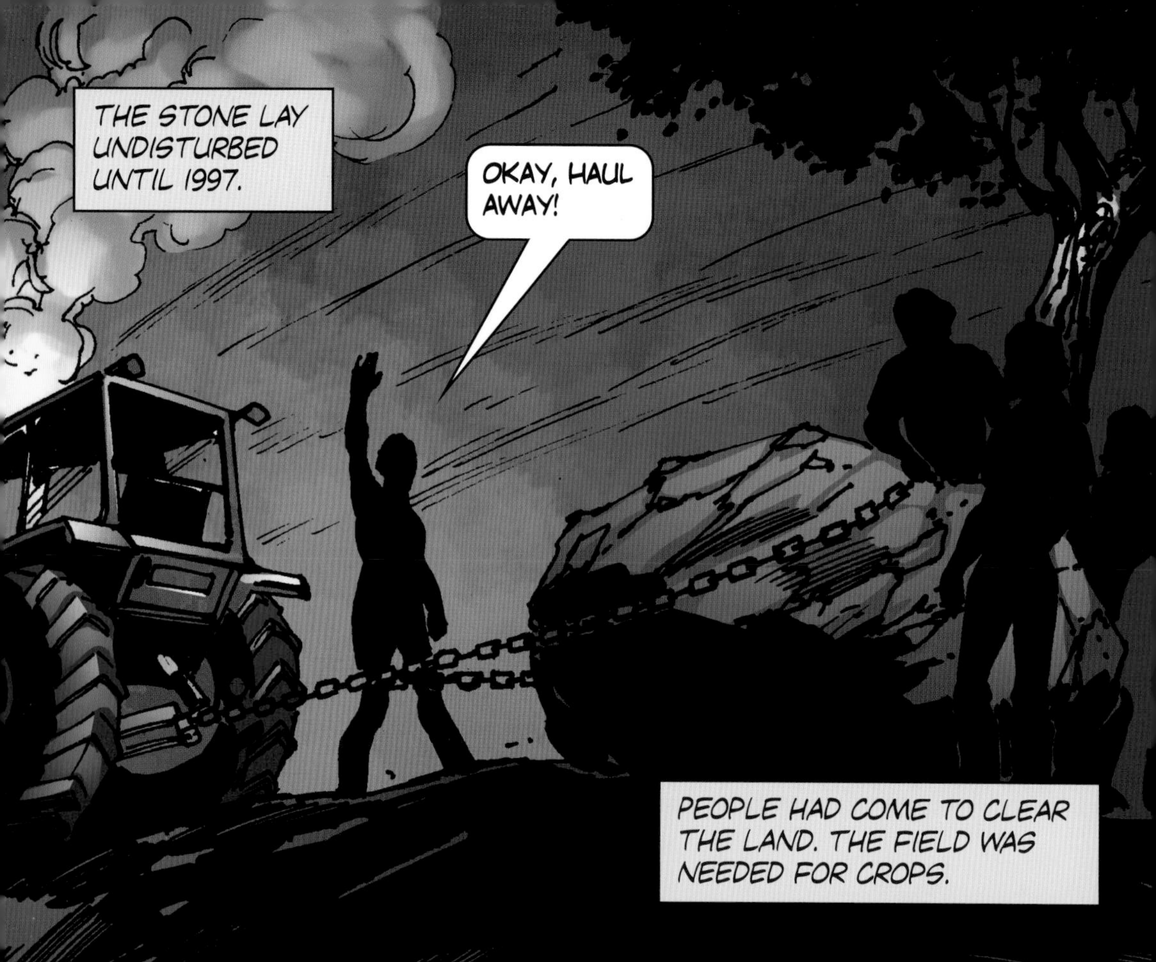
THE STONE LAY UNDISTURBED UNTIL 1997.
OKAY, HAUL AWAY!
PEOPLE HAD COME TO CLEAR THE LAND. THE FIELD WAS NEEDED FOR CROPS.

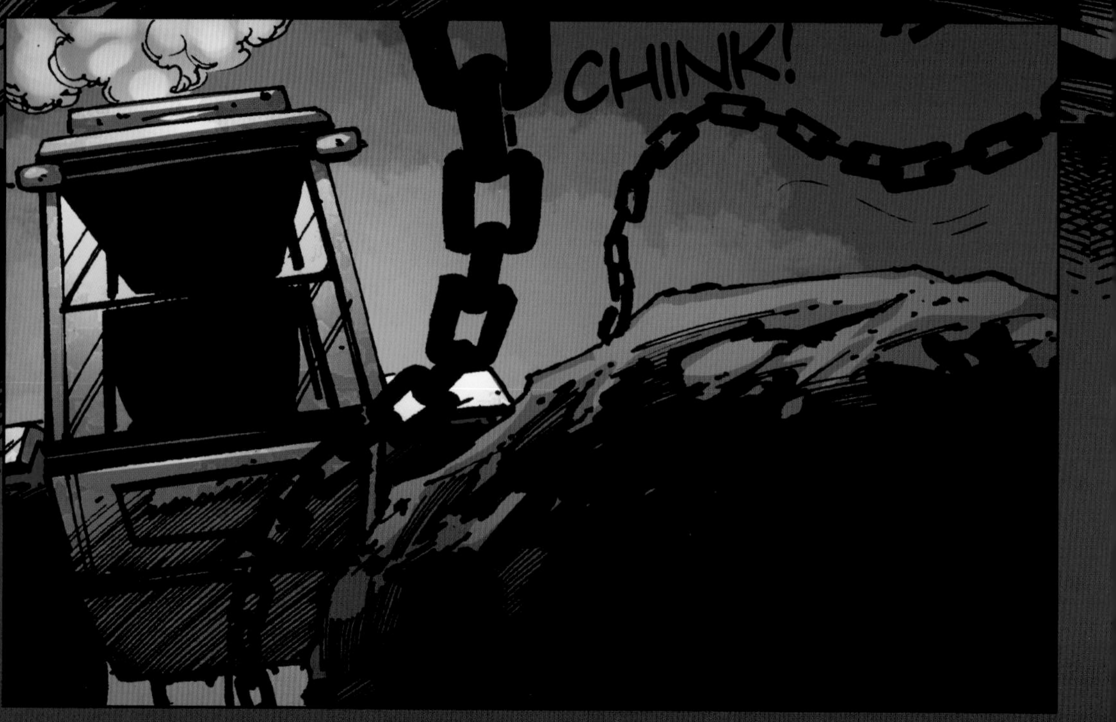
CHINK!

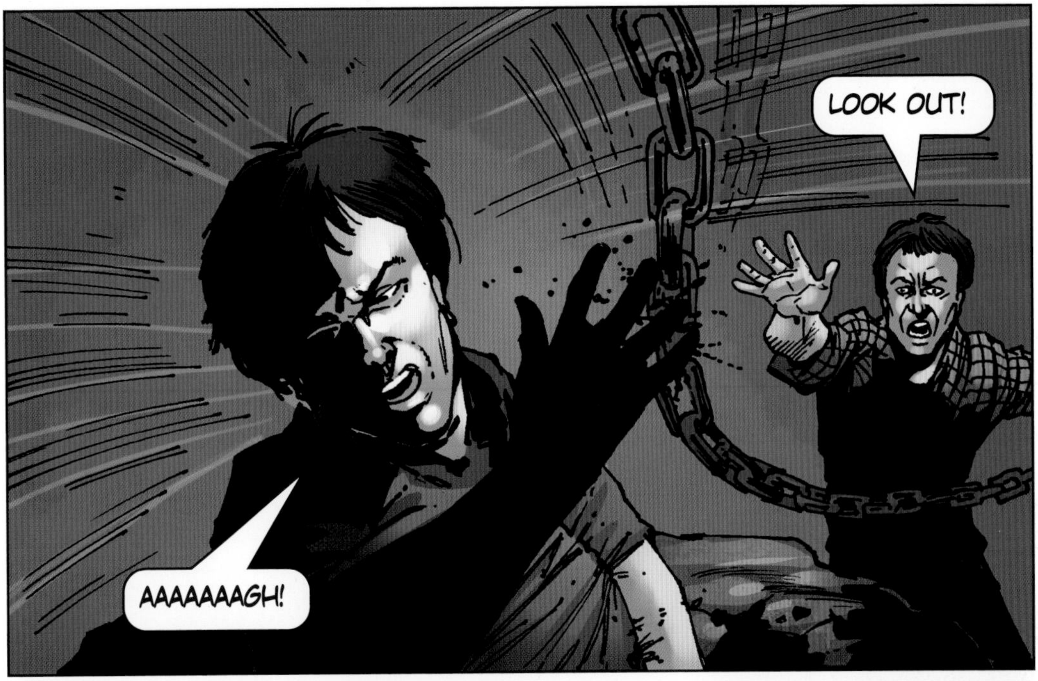
LOOK OUT!
AAAAAAAGH!

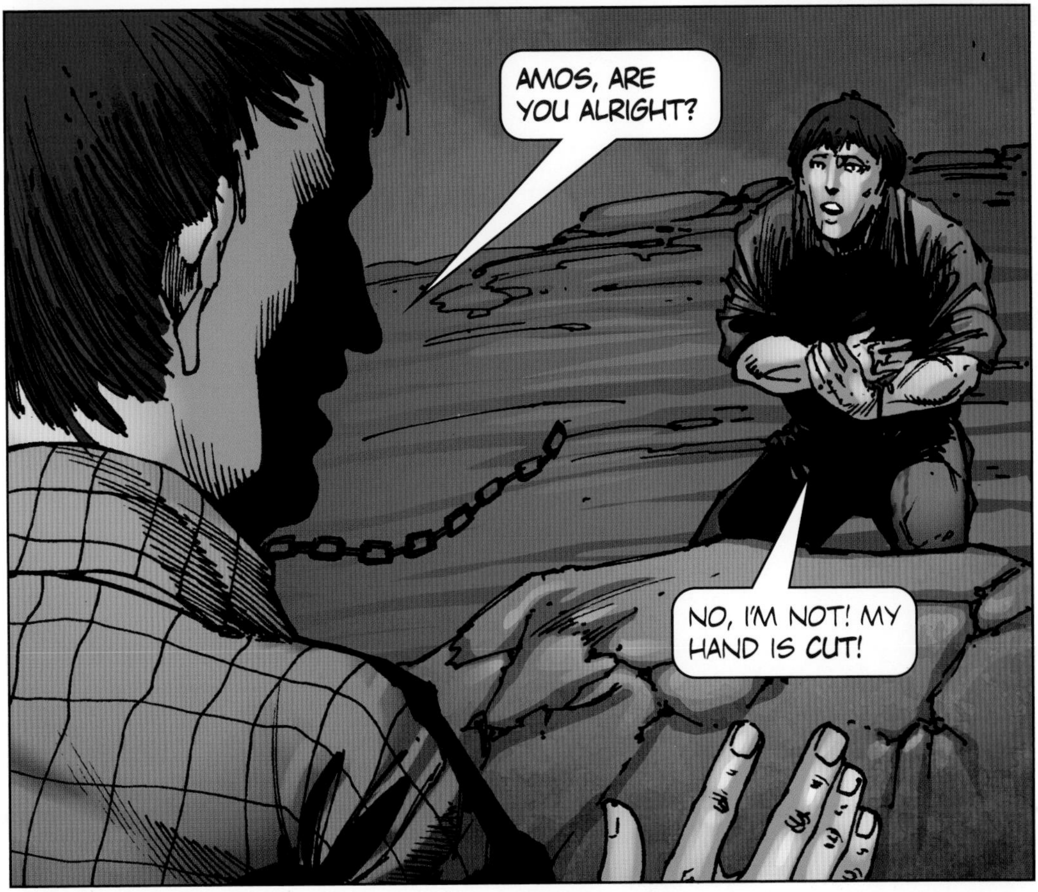
AMOS, ARE YOU ALRIGHT?
NO, I'M NOT! MY HAND IS CUT!

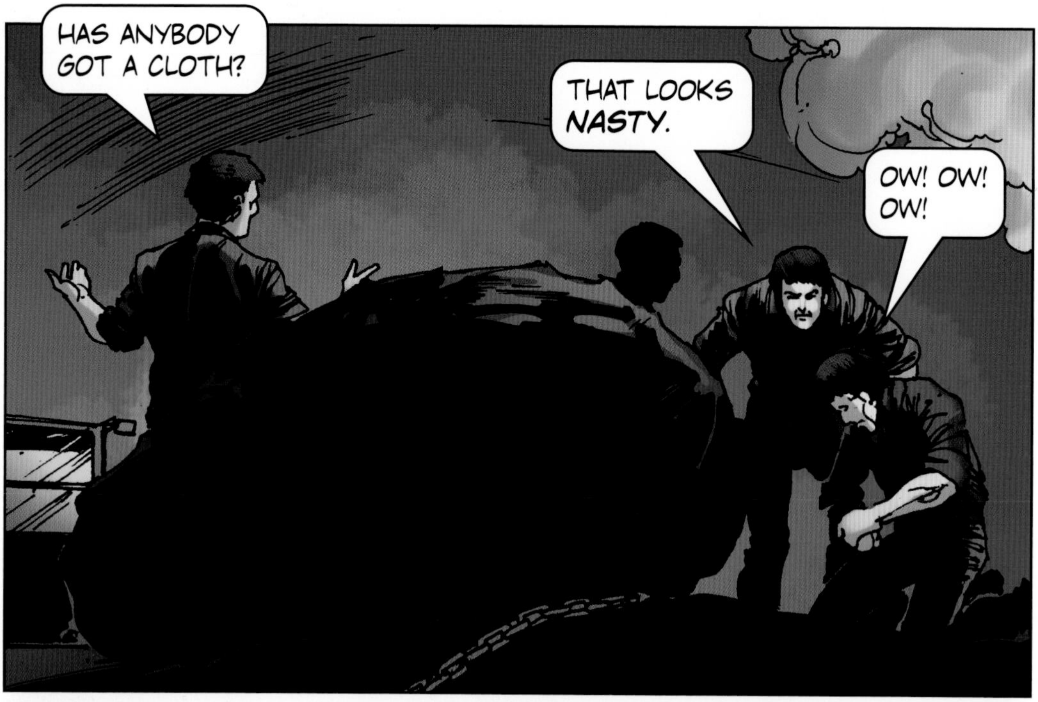
HAS ANYBODY GOT A CLOTH?
THAT LOOKS NASTY.
OW! OW! OW!

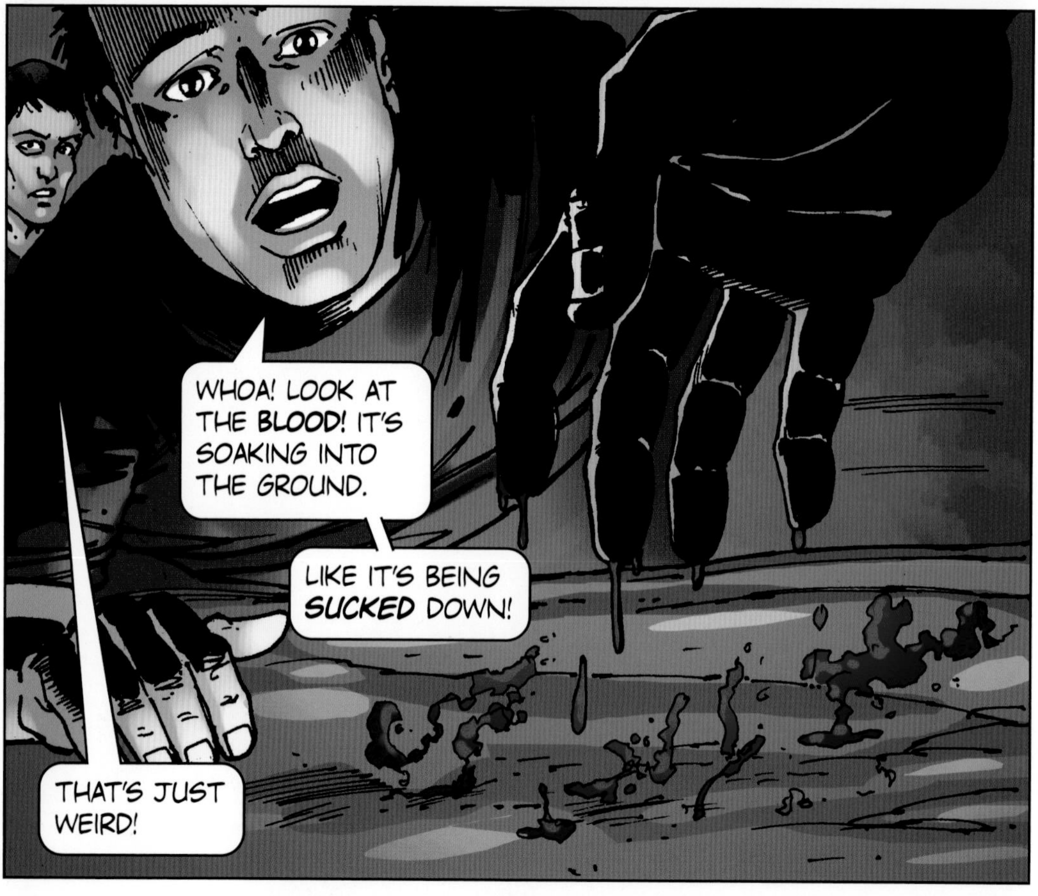
WHOA! LOOK AT THE BLOOD! IT'S SOAKING INTO THE GROUND.
LIKE IT'S BEING SUCKED DOWN!
THAT'S JUST WEIRD!

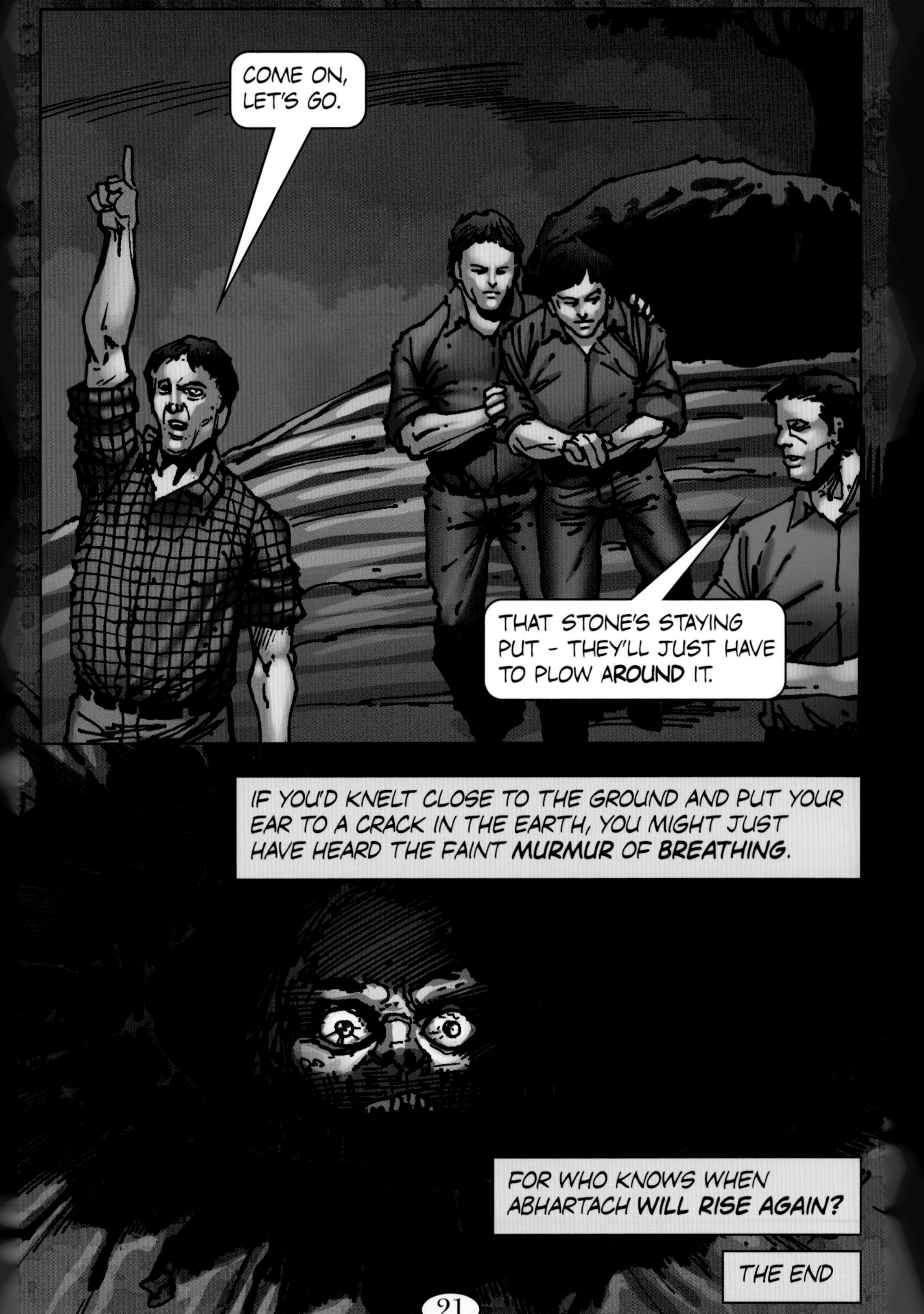
COME ON, LET'S GO.
THAT STONE'S STAYING PUT - THEY'LL JUST HAVE TO PLOW **AROUND** IT.
IF YOU'D KNELT CLOSE TO THE GROUND AND PUT YOUR EAR TO A CRACK IN THE EARTH, YOU MIGHT JUST HAVE HEARD THE FAINT ***MURMUR*** *OF* ***BREATHING.***
FOR WHO KNOWS WHEN ABHARTACH ***WILL RISE AGAIN?***
THE END

They burn in sunlight. They can be beheaded. They can be killed with silver—in folklore there is always a way to defeat a vampire. However, the battle is *not* for the fainthearted...

A suspected vampire is killed by a stake through the heart.

The Vampire of Croglin Grange

A woman moves into a new home in 17th-century England, only to be terrorized and bitten by a hideous ghoul. The ghoul is shot by her brothers but escapes. They trace its origin to a nearby churchyard. In the crypt lies a mummified body with a musket ball embedded in its leg.

A Plague of Vampires

In 18th-century Serbia, a whole village seems infected by vampirism. Year-old graves have been opened. The bodies are pink and fresh. Information points to a man named Arnont Paule, who had claimed he'd cured himself of a vampire's bite. The twist is that Paule had murdered the villagers *after* he had died in an accident. Twelve of his victims are hastily burnt before they, too, can rise.

Mercy Brown—the Last American Vampire

Exeter, Rhode Island, 1891. Mercy Brown dies, aged 19, from tuberculosis. Her elder brother, Edwin, also sick from the disease, dreams that Mercy has returned and is trying to kill him. With so many deaths in the area, the townfolk suspect Mercy is a life-sucking vampire. They open her coffin. Sure enough, she looks plump and fresh—more alive than she did in life. Her bleeding heart is cut out and burnt. From the ashes, a potion is made and given to Edwin, but it doesn't save him.

Glossary

corpse A dead body, usually of a human being.

demon An evil supernatural being, a devil.

druid A member of an order of priests in ancient Britain who appear in legends as prophets and sorcerers.

folklore Traditional beliefs, myths and tales that are passed down through generations by word of mouth.

ghoul An evil spirit, especially one that robs graves and eats dead bodies.

haul To pull or drag with effort or force.

immortal Unable to die.

legends Traditional stories often regarded as historical but not proven to be true.

musket ball The ammunition for a smoothbore shoulder gun that was used from the 16th through the 18th century.

shape-shift To alter one's physical appearance, usually in order to trick someone else.

slain To have been killed violently.

tuberculosis An infectious and often deadly disease.

Index